Little Steven Needs Our Help

Esmeralda Leal

ISBN 978-1-64114-833-7 (paperback)
ISBN 978-1-64114-834-4 (digital)

Christian Faith Publishing, Inc.
832 Park Avenue
Meadville, PA 16335
www.christianfaithpublishing.com

Printed in the United States of America

Dedicated to my Lord and Savior *Jesus Christ.*

It was a beautiful morning in Forest Hill;

all was quiet.

Little Claire and little Joy were asleep in their cozy bed.

Suddenly, they were awakened by voices and all kinds of noises just outside their window. Quickly, they ran to the window to look, and it was clear to see that they have new neighbors.

"Wow, new neighbors," cried little Joy.

"It's about time! Let's get ready and go meet them," said little Claire.

The new neighbors were busy moving boxes and unpacking. "What a beautiful place this is. I just love it," said the Mom.

"Yes," said Dad. "I just hope my little Steven will like it here too."

"Good morning and welcome to the neighborhood. I'm Claire, and this is my little sister Joy. We're your new neighbors."

"Hi, I'm Robert, and this is my little brother Steven."

Little Steven was wearing large headphones with no sound coming from them. The only sound was the loud humming he was making.

"Why is he wearing headphones and making that humming noise?" asked little Joy.

"Don't be rude," cried little Claire.

"Oh, it's OK. I rather she asks than just stare at him like everyone else does," said Robert. "My brother is autistic; that's why he hums. Right now, he's upset because we lost his toy cart during the move to our new home."

"We've never met someone who's autistic. What is that anyway?" asked little Joy.

"It's hard to explain. I guess you could say it affects your brain. Someone with autism may have problems with hearing, seeing, and even touching things. Also, they may not be able to taste certain foods. Sometimes, they have a hard time learning and expressing themselves. They also get attached to certain things that they can't be without. For example, little Steven can't go anywhere without his toys. He will cry and cry, and just have a hard time if he can't take them with him. This makes it hard for my parents to go places sometimes. We are used to hearing him hum, but others may find it unpleasant. It is also very difficult for him to make friends even with me, his own brother."

Little Claire got an idea. "Robert, maybe we can make your brother a new toy cart. Please come with us so you can meet all our friends. We'll get everyone together to build your little brother a new cart. I'm sure that together, we can do it!"

So off they went. Little Claire knew that they would all work together and make a good team, everybody doing their part.

Team work!

First, they went to meet Ally, Audrey, Anthony, and Sierra. They like feeding everyone, and they make the most delicious lemonade and sandwiches.

Next, they went to meet Antonio and Zachary. They enjoy building things when they are not outside playing ball. "Maybe one day you can come play ball with us," said Antonio.

"Sounds like fun," said Robert.

Next, they met Solara, Mia, Angelina, and Aiden. They enjoy visiting all the neighbors, and of course, they always share their sweet honey.

Then they met Maddox, Mercer, and Revelynn. They like visiting the neighbors and making sure there is no one in need of anything. "I can't wait to visit with you and your family," said Revelynn.

And finally, up they went to meet Little John and Little Aaron. They lived high up in a beautiful tree. They are always there when you need

them. They share their home with Joey, Asher, and Joseph who also keep watch on the neighborhood.

"Wow! You really can see everything from up here. I think I'm really going to like it here. Everyone I've meet is really nice," said Robert.

"I knew you would like it here," said little Joy "We'll have so much fun!" She exclaimed!

"Let's get everyone together and come up with ideas to help little Steven," said little Claire.

So everyone got together and met little Steven and were even more eager to come up with a plan to help him. They knew little Steven needed to take his toys everywhere he went. To make things easier for the family, they decided to build little Steven a new toy cart so he could carry most of his toys anywhere he went.

So the next day, they went looking for all the supplies they would need. "This is going to be fun," said Robert. "I'm sure he will love his toy cart," said little Joy.

Up from the sky, John and Aaron would guide everyone through the forest. Wood and vines were plentiful, so they gathered all the supplies they needed.

The next day, they all got together to build the toy cart, even little Steven got involved. He lined up his toys ready to be put into his cart. Mom made cookies for everyone, and Dad supervised everyone, making sure no one got hurt. "Now this is team work," said Mom.

The next day, after all the hard work they had done, they all decided to go to the pond for a day of fun with all their new friends. Little Steven was very happy with his new toy cart. Mom and Dad were also very happy that they had moved to such a wonderful neighborhood.

The day at the pond was so much fun.

Mom and Dad were so happy that little Steven and Robert had met such caring and helpful friends.

About the Author

Hello, my name is Esmeralda M. Leal; and for the last nine years, I have worked as a Paraprofessional in a life skills class. My school district has sent me to special education workshops throughout the years, and I have learned so much in this area. I have had the privilege of working with amazing teachers and paraprofessionals. Working as a team with my coworkers benefits all our students and promotes a good learning environment. When I come home from a long day of work, I relax by reading and drawing. I try to garden when I have time. On weekends, I'm in charge of the nursery at my church, which I absolutely love.